I0673682

Will And Resistance

Lawrence Johns

Published by Conscious Publishing, 2024.

WILL AND RESISTANCE

First edition. January 15, 2024.

ISBN: 978-1929096077

Written by Lawrence Johns.

Table of Contents

for MFJ

The Fountains Of Darkness

Metis watches the ripples

Created by descending geese

Slowly spread across the twilight pond

As he closes white linen curtains

And aligns the V Dome

In the middle of the maple floor

He's instantly back on Porth

In the high cave overlooking

A red sandstone canyon

And its wide cobalt river

Winding through cottonwoods

He calls it Slingshot

His accelerator of Intent

Discovered on a previous Exploration

And furnished Victorian

Dense with smells of burnished oak

Old vellum

And Shetland wool

A glass globe on a brass stand

Marking Magellan's crooked route

Around Earth's rough continents

Slowly spins in witness

As Metis brings his breathing down

Enters a second Voletic Meditation

And goes Outside the World

His first View is a Luminous Pearl

Bending all surrounding Space

Into a black satin pillow

Supporting its radiant Beauty

His second View depicts our Universe

As a molecule in a Dodecahedron

Hovering motionless in the Void

He's seen these Outside Views before

So Metis presses on

Deeper into the Darkness

Looking for a new Creation Story

He's walking Seven-League Boots

With the earthy pleasure of feet

Pounding stubborn soil

In a brisk banjo rhythm

He's whistling a bluegrass tune

To confound the preternatural Silence

When he comes to a Well of Blackness

A violent Vortex spinning clockwise

Below the invisible Surface

His Observation triggers Eruption

A Fountain of Energy

Rises from deep Underneath

Hesitates

Then creates small balls of Light

Where it crashes to the ground

After resuming his long strides

Metis encounters more Fountains

Ejected from a Body so massive

It exceeds mathematical Scale

Each Light is a new World

A bubble swept away in perfect Liquid

Accelerated outward by the following Crash

He's analyzing the Expansion pattern

In his Advanced Mind

When he's suddenly back in Slingshot

Decompressing in woolly geometry

Sketching in his Exploration Log

4

And anticipating Gwendyllian's embrace

Waiting sweet and witty at the cabin

After his jump back to Earth

Amethyst Eyes

At thirteen Kendra

Of the amethyst eyes

And strawberry blonde hair

Discovers she can talk to the Sun

She learns the emotional History

Of the solar system

How the Sun was separated

From her Twin Sister

Shortly after Lighting Up

How she wandered lonely

Before she found a safe Void

Between two large spiral arms

To raise her family of planets

In those early Violent Times

Major disasters were frequent

Daughter Five

Exploded into a billion fragments

Close to Jupiter

And the life-giving water

On Venus and Mars evaporated

Leaving them sullenly sterile

The Sun felt weak and helpless

When the rogue planet Saturn

Bristling with baleful Hate

Dropped into orbit from Nowhere

And started the Nightmares

As a young plasma Mother

The Sun's original hopes

For her Daughters

Were constantly tested

By the bombardment

Of erratic comets and asteroids

So she felt a special pleasure

When Daughter Three

Transformed mother's flares into Life

Developed a molten iron Spin

Inside her Big Heart

And a strong magnetic Halo

To protect Life's Progress

University professors can't decide

If Kendra has a rare paranormal Gift

Or has found a way to integrate

The voletic and electromagnetic

Quantum Fields

In her precocious Advanced Mind

Kendra has early Notice

Of magnetic storms

Supernovae

And other major Cosmic Events

Long before they approach Earth

And at seventeen Kendra

Of the sparkling eyes

Harmonious Form

And braided long blonde hair

Enters the Derwid Council

At twenty

Her first Explorations

Are models of Efficiency and Tact

After talking to a Red Giant

In the Milky Way

She learns the Andromeda Galaxy

Was formed from molecular clouds

Without any type of Water

Any possibility of Life

Exploring the Local Filament

Through the Virgo

Vela

And Shapley Superclusters

Towards the Great Attractor

She finds a total absence of Sentience

And must push far into The Deep

Before meeting a gregarious Main Sequence

Singing the praises of Daughter Four

In a temperate zone of liquid Water

The planet is oxygenated by large forests

And networked with Oosmos

An orange underground fungus

That pushes up trillions of brown knobs

To the moist and leafy Surface

After analyzing its chemical composition

Kendra discovers that a single knob

Supplies fifty times the daily protein

And other nutrients needed by Man

So Kendra asks permission

Of the chatty standard Star

Takes a detailed scan of Oosmos

With her ultra-violet eyes

And returns to Earth

Channeling her Excitement

Into the first twelve Oosmos recipes

Lucky

Ruggiero consistently asserts

To his alternating Self-Identities

That good Fortune flows directly

From good Preparation and Persistence

So when he joins in the search

For the legendary Red Filament

And its hundred billion White Pyramids

He first makes a map of the Cosmic Web

And projects candidate locations

Onto its spherical coordinates

After decades of frustrating Explorations

The standard depiction of the Web

As a fat filling Sponge

Seems an antiquated Convenience

A simple Contrivance to him now

The orthodox structure

Of Filaments and Voids

Doesn't match the disparate mix

Of Information and Illusion

That continues to frustrate his Desire

To activate the White Pyramids

And build out the Cosmic Brain

Ruggiero's Explorations

Have produced a High Strangeness

That makes every Observation suspect

And puzzles his Advanced Mind

The closer he looks at the Web

The closer it clumps

And bounces randomly between

Being and Non Being

The more he filters new Experiences

The more the selections spoil his plans

And leave him frustrated and confused

To break this Paralysis

Ruggiero chooses the Territory

Over the Map

This Filament running before him

Could Be the Red Filament

So it Is

He overrides the Probabilities

And immediately gets Lucky

Slipping down through orange clouds

To a steep mountain range

He spots a White Pyramid

On a high plateau

From Distance

It looks like another Shell

Another empty promise

Mocking a century of Explorations

And High Expectations

After touchdown

Ruggiero enters the Pyramid

And climbs to the viewing platform

No sounds

No motion

Nothing

Just more bitter evidence

Of the increasingly futile Search

The number of galaxies and planets

In the Universe is simply too large

To Build the Brain

By Increment or Chance

Ruggiero walks melancholy

Out of the Pyramid

And finds a gray slate rock

Twenty yards away in the fluffy dust

I'm the Prime Observer!

He shouts

I'm watching You!

I'm interacting with You

You can't be Anything anymore!

You're the Cosmic Brain

Start working!

Nothing happens

So Ruggiero rings the bell

Returns Home

And rehearses some new lines

The next afternoon

He's sitting on the same rock

Confronting the Pyramid

I'm watching You

With the Eyes of Eternity

Start working!

Start working Now!

For seventeen days straight

Ruggiero sits and addresses

The White Pyramid

With crescendos of Flattery

And cogent Persuasion

On the eighteenth day

After the first few syllables

It emits a loud hum

And like a human Synapse

Begins accepting

And rejecting Information

From other Pyramids

Ruggiero laughs

And takes a slow jubilant walk

Around the lucky structure in the dust

Repeating every ninety degrees

It's working

The Universe will soon be Conscious

It's working

The Universe will soon be Conscious

The Seventh Note

Beautiful Gwendyllian

Selects the honeysuckle print dress

From the cherrywood armoire

And evaluates her reflection

In the beveled Welsh mirror

Yes

Just the right look

To find the Infant God

She pins up her rich ebony hair

Drapes the emerald necklace

Across her breasts

And fastens its golden clasp

Securely behind her neck

She pulls the three-legged chair

To the center of the V Dome space

And after four deep breaths

She's exploring a purple beach

In a small desolate Cove

With a brackish brown sea

Lapping mean to the shore

She feels the maliciousness

Of two red Suns

Angled high in the Sky

She sees an Eagle flapping

Falling back

Then leaping again

Trying to escape

An invisible Trap

It's Iggy

A young boy pounding unseen bars

With his fists

Shocked to see the Infant God

So soon

Gwendyllian jumps back

To her cottage

Fingering her necklace

And taking a moment to recover

How did Iggy get captured?

What possible Force

Could hold him there?

And Why?

Then she's back to the beach

And Iggy's a Puma

Growling and clawing

At the foul purple sand

She tries to spring the Trap

With emergency Solutions

Stored in her Advanced Mind

But nothing works

So Gwendyllian flies inland

Desperate for help

The Ugliness of the beach

Is stark counterpoint

To a gorgeous tropical planet

Covered by green and yellow canopies

Vibrating with high-pitched Calls

Gwendyllian alights on a limb

And addresses a Congress of Songbirds

Displaying a flaming palette of feathers

Please help me!

I have to free Iggy!

Gwendyllian pleads

He's trapped on the beach

Please come!

The Birds stop singing

And fly to the canopy to confer

When they return

They speak sympathetically

Telepathically

We've lost many Young Beauties

To these horrible Traps

But after long Investigation

We finally found the Note

That opens the Sonic Cages

Come then!

Come with me!

We never leave the Forest

Then please teach me the Note!

The Birds form a psychedelic helmet

Around her head

Chanting

Sing the seven ascending notes

Of the Bhairav raga

Then the seven descending notes

Omitting the third

Repeat the ascending notes as before

Then the descending again

This time omitting the fifth

Sing the ascending scale once more

Omitting the Seventh and Final Note

The Infinite Power of Silence

Will then open the Sonic Trap

Gwendyllian thanks the Birds

Flies back to the fetid beach

And sings the scales

Pitched three octaves down

For her human throat

After the penultimate note fades

Into the dismal background

There's a loud Crack

And the struggling Infant God

Flies Up

Out of Sight

Rhodri's Announcement

When Rhodri approaches the granite Podium

On the Museum Theater stage

Radiating stout Gravitas

And smoothing his auburn moustache

The large Audience knows

Something is Up

Rhodri records every Face

With glacier blue eyes

Takes a quick sip of water

From a green crystal tumbler

And begins to thunder

This evening we honor

Four outstanding Sagaxi

Their Discoveries in The Deep

Will accelerate our Knowledge

Of the Universe and Ourselves

They've taken the Western Way

To distant Planets

Imprinted their Personalities

Into the fabric of Spacetime

And returned with new Ideas

To make Athenapolis shine brighter

My Fellow Derwids

As we approach the 50th Athenaid

Of our Serene City

As we commend the Talent

And Resourcefulness

Of these four Explorers

We honor the Foresight and Courage

Of the Founders

When they threw off

The Military Political Apparatus

Of the Commerce Class

Broke the Nation State Hegemony

And announced the Extraordinary Individual

As the Goal of Society

They set a course for the Unknown

For a dynamic new Social Contract

Where Western Enlightenment rules

And Society is a study in Self-Perfection

They painted a Landscape of Inspiration

Where great artistic Creations

And scientific Inventions

Arise spontaneously

In conversations between Friends

Walking in our splendid gardens

Rhodri pauses three beats

Takes another sip of water

And addresses the State of the City

My fellow Derwids

For the first time in Human History

The Founders created a Society

Committed to the Freedom

Brought by Lasting Peace

And the High Culture created

By competition between Advanced Minds

Our founders were Visionaries

But they couldn't anticipate

The petty philosophical debates

The compounded civic lethargy

And the lack of erotic stimulation

Resulting from a hundred years

Of unchallenged Universal Peace

Today the City is reluctant

To leave the warm and perfumed bath

Of her Advanced Knowledge

And take the necessary Risks

To test and improve accepted Truths

In the velvet grip of Convention

Poetry has slid into confessions

Physics has lapsed into reinterpretations

Of orthodox theories and old computer data

And the horses I bring to the Festival

Win with progressively worse times

Over increasingly inferior competition

My fellow Derwids

Look Outside

And look Inside

The Signs are Everywhere

After forty-nine Athenaids

The City has sunk into Ennui

And intractable Homeostasis

Our Serenity has become fossilized

By its Success

Athenapolis rescued Earth

From Nuclear Destruction

And Climate Catastrophe

But twenty-two thousand years

Of modest and tedious Survival

Is not our chosen Destiny

We refuse to allow the great Victory

Achieved by the Founders

To decay into common Entropy

And vapid intellectual Consensus

When Giorgio Colli investigated

Nietzsche's unpublished notes

He discovered why our Great Ally

Never finished The Will To Power

And the Reason

Is found in Three Will Theory

Without strong Resistance

First Will eventually fatigues

Weakens

And creates Second Will

All Being

Then longs for Non Being

And this longing becomes manifest

In a thousand bitter Denunciations

And Renunciations of Life

That all end in senseless Death

My fellow Derwids

This evening in our Museum Theater

I ask for your Genius

I ask for your Assistance

Athenapolis has become Pale and Normalized

A Caricature and Satire of Herself

The Restoration saved Earth from Disaster

And Man from Self-Extinction

But the Lasting Peace

Has made us soft and vulnerable

In her oblivious and weakened Condition

Athenapolis is swift and easy Prey

For any Alien Predator from The Deep

With superior Technology

Or any well-organized internal Enemy

Commanded by Second Will

And supported by Artificial Intelligence

Our Physical Energy is crippled

By the absence of a True Emergency

Our Advanced Minds are atrophied

By the absence of a Sharp Dialectic

My fellow Derwids

The darkest line on the Graph

Is the City's falling birthrate

Due to slacking erotic Passion

The number of Babies is down

The number of Explorations is down

The number of Continuations is way down

We're declining

Decaying

Dissolving

Into an Ocean of Meaninglessness

Into a Cup of Contentment

Listen my Sagaxi

The Council has made the Difficult Decision

This evening I announce War

You're the Next Men

You're the most Extraordinary Individuals

The Earth has ever seen

Now you're Called to Arms

Now you're asked to strengthen

The Alliance of First and Third Will

By starting a Rebellion

That will guarantee our Peace

Athenapolis is a Nietzschean Project

Based on Dangerous Ideas

Use one to organize the Resistance

Go to your labs and studios

Create the Chaos and Deception

That gets Athenapolis back on track

And forces the First Will Imperative

Into immediate and decisive Action

My Sagaxi

We must be Stronger!

Bring the City to her Knees!

As Rhodri roars this last line

The lights suddenly go out

And the Audience is forced to exit

Feeling for each other's arms

And calling out to their children

The Oosmos Diet

The Restoration returned Earth

To predictable and benign Seasons

Volcanic eruptions

Droughts

And floods were rare

The massive tree planting Projects

Organized and conducted by Homoborgs

Were supplemented by a network

Of Grand Canals

That vitalized the deserts and steppes

Without global Conflict

Economic Strife

And environmental Disaster

Earth was once again a Garden

And Man the fastidious Caretaker

Of her verdant Magnificence

To Kendra the overthrow

Of the Commerce Class

Was validated by the success

Of the City's ecology programs

The Wilderness was restored

To its primeval Logic

And many endangered Species

Quickly returned to healthy populations

In Kendra

The provocations of Rhodri

Produced spasms of Anxiety

That twisted her inner organs

Into tight and painful knots

After a century of Peace

And consistent progress towards

Environmental Health

Athenapolis will soon be at War

So she quickens her pace

And conducts scientific experiments

That prove Oosmos

Puts more useful chemicals

Into the soil than it extracts

And significantly enhances the growth

Of neighboring trees and vegetation

After five-esteemed Chefs

Report that Oosmos

Is more delicious and versatile

Than all traditional protein sources

Kendra closes the fisheries

And stops the slaughter of livestock

Everywhere on Earth

Some chickens are kept for eggs

Some cattle and goats are kept for milk

Some sheep for wool

All remaining domesticated animals

Save dogs and cats

Are transported back to the Wild

No longer will Man

Eat the flesh of his fellow Creatures

Oosmos is more nutritious

Than a ribeye roast

More irresistible

Than coconut chocolate pudding

With one Discovery from the Deep

Kendra creates a new Diet

And a new civic Virtue

She removes the Deep Stain

Of animal Sacrifice

Conducted by Sapiens Priests

And the horrific breeding conditions

Instituted by the Commerce Class

With one gastronomic Innovation

In a Moment of High Tension

Kendra strengthens

The Health and Pride of the City

Before the Enemy is identified and engaged

The Copper Cubes

———

When the Artist sees a Concept

Actualized to Perfection

When the Artwork is so sublime

It reaches back in Time

To create itself

The emotional High is so strong

That the Artist wants to carry

This exhilarating Momentum

Into the next composition

Because every Masterpiece

Requires an original Vision

That disrupts the norms of Perception

The Insight expressed in the Original

Must be given a different Vector

When it flows into the Next

The success of the Oosmos Diet

Moved Kendra to collaborate

With Metis in the Theory

Design

And Construction of machinery

To convert Voletic Energy

Into unlimited electrical Power

For all thirty-three thousand iterations

Of Athenapolis

Their late night research

In the University Labs

And brainstorming Dialogs

Walking through fragrant orange groves

Produced a new technology

Using the Earth's immense Velocity

Hurtling through the Cosmic Voletic Field

To transform voletrons into electrons

And provide an inexhaustible Power Source

For all the City's electricity needs

Kendra and Metis supervise the completion

Of the eighty-foot tall

Gleaming Copper Cubes

That house the transformers

And produce changing Solar Reflections

To Man's first application of Free Energy

Now the City can extend the power Grid

To cover every inch of Earth

Now the City has endless electricity

To conduct and win the War

And now

After two Masterpieces of Positive Art

The Artist rests

The Puya Flower

He's sliding his last bite

Of buckwheat pancake

Through a dot of maple syrup

When he feels Gwendyllian's smile

Light up the kitchen

Today's The Day

No words

No gestures

Just that big smile

Illuminating the imminent Hunt

They've been talking for months

About hiking the Lafferty Mountains

Searching for the Flower

Of the legendary Puya plant

That blooms once a century

He readies their backpacks

A train

Two busses

A trailhead

And three hours later

Metis and Gwendyllian

Are making Love

On a lime green sleeping pad

Overlooking a slender stream

Dancing down from the Lafferties

They brought a pup tent

But find a ledge leading to a cave

Easily protected by a small fire

That becomes Home Base

For day trips seeking the Flower

They spot some mature plants

On the higher ridges

But no buds or blooms

And every hike is frequently interrupted

By impromptu Ecstasies

Escaping from warm shallow pools

And soft forest bowers

Of pine needles and fallen leaves

On their last night

After tending a blaze on the ledge

To frustrate the intentions

Of the hungry night Predators

Metis enters the cave

And sees Gwendyllian

Pointing her flashlight

At the outlines of red hands

Surrounding a white spot

On the rough ceiling

Love

Look at this!

The Wrath Of Achilles

A dissonant Rumor

Circulates in the City

Claiming the Noble Class

Is allowing Duels

To settle internal disputes

So Ruggiero goes to investigate

With his new friend Dalarick

The muscular Marquis de Bohemond

Receives them in the Herald Hall

Of his crumbling marble Chateau

With a crisp and diffident Air

And a demi-tasse of golden cognac

After the usual prolonged niceties

The Marquis dismisses

His apprehensive butler

And launches into a monolog

On the state of the City

My esteemed Guests

One of the founding Principles

Of the Serene City we share

Is the Extraordinary Individual

The Man so distinguished

By Breeding and Rank

That his Superbia

Is a constant spur to others

Jealous of his Fame and Social Status

Like the Struggle

Between Achilles and Agamemnon

And the long War

Between Athens and Sparta

The ancient Rule of Rank

Necessarily provokes Insults

Rage

And culminates in Revenge

This repeating cycle

From Insult to Vengeance

Played out in the annals of History

Is the true Western Way

As expressed in our finest Literature

And most important Wars

Since we destroyed the Neanderthals

40

Forty thousand years ago

The Noble Class has defended

The Virility Of Man

Against luxurious Eastern Assault

Against rampant internal Decadence

With stern and consistent Resolve

My Derwids

With the Wisdom Class in Power

We have no Rank

We have no Justice

We have no Progress

Every Action is a Sublimation

Of the Wrath of Achilles

That results in sickly Quiescence

The Nobility understands

The defense of Personal Honor

As the highest Motivation for Man

The Nobility understands

Western Culture

As the Highest and Best Expression

Of Vengeance

The Marquis lets these words

Echo through long Herald Hall

Then leans over and says

Sotto voce

At a cheery cocktail hour

The Duke of Lucca

Made salacious and defamatory remarks

About a translation of Anacreon

Written by the Duke of Dusseldorf

The Challenge was immediately sent

The choice of weapons was Foils

And the Duel took place in predawn fog

On a wet and wide sandbank

Across the Missouri River

Despite extended ministrations

The Seconds were unable

To elicit an Apology

The Duke of Lucca repeated his Slander

And the Duel correctly began

Dusseldorf started with a feint

That offered Lucca an opening

For an attack in quatre

Which Dusseldorf parried of tierce

And quickly disengaged

Providing a second opening for attack

Then as Lucca defended a false thrust

Dusseldorf turned his wrist

Raised his foil two inches

And punctured Lucca's throat

The Marquis sighs

Drops to the floor

To execute twenty quick pushups

And finishes with a final sip

Of his amber cognac

This could set a Precedent

Says Ruggiero

If Duels become fashionable

In the Noble Class

They could spread like plague

To the other Classes

We prefer to let Fate or God

Decide these matters

Replies de Behemond

The Restoration gave Power

To the wrong Class

You Derwids are mongrels and mutants

Ambitious bastards obsessed with Power

That happened to stumble

Upon a Weapon

In a rare window of opportunity

The Noble Class ruled for millennia

Before the Commerce Class

And we shall rule again

After the Revolution

The World can't live without Rank

Or the spilling of blood

In the defense of Honor

The Marquis de Bohemond

Closes the Interview

By pointing his forefinger

At Ruggiero's chest

If you be Men

My Second awaits your Challenge

As they walk carefully down

The steep marble steps

Ruggiero whispers to Dalarick

You didn't say a word

Blow winds and crack your cheeks!

Dalarick recites

The Silver Tokens

———

One Tuesday small silver tokens

Started appearing in the City

First placed on restaurant tables

And scattered on public transportation

Then surfacing in cars and homes

Each disc was inscribed

Redeem for $1000

At First Citizens Bank

Money is unknown in Athenapolis

So the Silver Tokens were rightly seen

As shiny markers in a Game

Originating in the Player Class

And most found their way

Into pockets and dresser drawers

Out of simple Curiosity

Intrigued by the boldness of the Play

Ruggiero and Dalarick

Decide to investigate the Player Class

For the first Interview

They meet Lloyd Halpern

President of First Citizens Bank

In his warehouse Pod

Lloyd's wearing a gray T-shirt

Sporting thick blonde stubble

And squeezing a small plastic ball

Welcome Derwids!

Bring your Tokens?

All Early Birds

Get in at the Ground Floor

Of the New American Revolution

Ruggiero and Dalarick

Round up a pair of office chairs

And watch Lloyd monitor

Eight large video screens

And bounce his purple ball

As he gives them the Pitch

You can redeem your Tokens

For Cash

Real Estate

Or blue-chip Stocks

And for every Million Dollar investment

You'll get a First Citizens hoodie

And a logo coffee cup

The response from Players and Nobles

Has been Off the Charts

And you Derwids

Haven't been shy jumping on

This astounding Business-Opportunity

As Lloyd briefly swivels

To make eye contact

Ruggiero asks

What's this all about?

The Token Con is so fundamental

You Derwids will never figure it out

Lloyd answers

Turning back to the screens

It's the confirmation of Greed and Envy

As the primary Motivators of Man

When someone finds a Token on the street

He immediately looks for more

And envies his Friends

Amassing a bigger stash

Through Luck or Guile

When you redeem your Tokens

Here at First Citizens Bank

You'll attract Wealth

You'll date beautiful Women

You'll leverage your holdings

Into hedge funds for billions

And retire before you're forty

My dear Friends

Maybe you came to hear this

Derwid Time is Over

The New American Revolution

Has launched a New American Dream

And First Citizens Bank is brokering

The City's transition to Advanced Capitalism

With the infallible assistance of A I

My dear Derwids

Every attempt at Socialism

Has ended in abject Failure

And created a new version of Totalitarianism

Without a chance at personal Dominance

In a money-based Society

Man becomes anesthetized

Depressed

And indifferent to Survival

Like the drunken New Man

Of the original Soviet Union

Athenapolis is the current entry

In the ignominious list of Wretched Losers

Beginning with the Russian Revolution

You even have the Nerve

To call it the Western Way

In Fact

It's the most preposterous Eastern Way

In the History of the World

Lloyd laughs

As he bounces the ball high

Towards the steel rafters

Of the repurposed warehouse

And catches it in a platinum cup

Nine inches from the floor

My dear distracted Derwids

All the Real Estate on Earth

Has already been Sold and Assigned

The New Owners will take Possession

Immediately after the Revolution

Greed and Envy are the Engines of Reality

The New American Revolution

And the rebirth of Free Capitalism

Means Early Birds will get rich

From the Inventions of the Derwids

And the Labor of the Homoborgs

I'm sure you both appreciate

The Socratic Irony of our Plan

Every Citizen that comes to us

To redeem a Silver Token

Affirms our Right to Revolt

And our Right to Rule

He understands the Necessity

Of regaining his Person as Private Property

And managing the Working Class

To produce maximum Profit

This smooth line charts the probability

Of the Wisdom Class falling

Within the next eighteen days

It's holding steady at 83%

And trending higher

First Citizens Bank

Has prepared a loan package

For every Citizen of the City

Who wants equity participation

In the New Athenapolis

Thousands of Players have already invested

With points from their Fantasy Leagues

My dear foolish Derwids

Your Good Will is your Credit

Take advantage while your Talents

Still have some market value

The loan application

Is already on your phones

Lloyd bounces the ball harder

On the raw concrete floor

And it vanishes into the Void

As his attention is fatally locked

By breaking news on the seventh screen

Weaving towards the Exit

Ruggierto watches the Players

Texting their clients

The odds and betting lines

On every Event happening in the City

Lloyd Halpern's attitude

Reveals a deep Ressentiment

That could transform any Accident

Or Misunderstanding

Into bloody Revolution

The Silvers Tokens are Trojan Horses

Engineered by gaming gurus

To infiltrate the Wisdom Class

With the ancient Odor of Wealth

And destroy Athenapolis

From Inside the Walls

Two hundred Players are taking bets

On the Fall of the Wisdom Class

With the probability now at 88%

When Ruggiero notices Dalarick's angry face

At the armored security doors

You're still not talking?

Rage! Blow!

You cataracts and hurricanes

Dalarick recites King Lear again

Rousseau

It's Friday morning

And the two Friends

Are analyzing their Interviews

At the Broken Cup

Over double expressos

The Marquis and Lloyd Halpern

Were predictably delusional

Ruggiero says

And available

Dalarick adds smiling

Ruggiero drips cream

Into a miniature cup

And resumes his conclusions

The Duels and Silver Tokens

Were effective Lures

To draw our Attention

But I didn't see any real Threat

Or working Organization

Their Revolution braggadocio

Is a mix of Fantasy and Compensation

For their reduced Status in Society

We've always assumed

Since the time of Carlos

That Revolution

Would spark in the Working Class

But no word or sign of Discontent

Has ever come from the Homoborgs

That in itself

Is a cause of Concern

Dalarick says

If Second and Third Will

Are operating through the Homoborgs

Without their knowledge or consent

And disguising all Revolutionary Intent

Until the Time is Right

The City could Blow

Without ever identifying the Leaders

Or their Sources

Might be time for an Investigation

Ruggiero says

Looking at his Omega watch

The bus to Suburbia stops here

In exactly sixteen minutes

After throwing their cups to the floor

And watching them shatter

The Friends ride a silent hour

To the vast Homoborg Sector

And park on a cedar bus bench

Watching cumulus clouds

Samba the baby blue sky

Everything looks pretty peaceful

Dalarick says sarcastically

As they scan the tight rows

Of single-family homes

With freshly mown lawns

And technicolor flower beds

Lining the clean streets

Were you expecting a robot ghetto?

Ruggiero asks

Homoborgs are 90% of the City

And Suburbia is the Showcase

Of the Restoration

Everybody's happy Here

They have Tranquility

And Practical Immortality

To illustrate his words

A long yellow bus rolls up

And discharges a cacophony of kids

Flying to the pool and playfields

Of Asimov Park

We need a Subject

Dalarick says

Anyone will do

Ruggiero answers

They're all One Mind

As they contemplate

The implications of this remark

A Homoborg walks up

Wearing a beige Latin shirt

Humming a Bennie Moten tune

And swinging a bowling ball bag

He stops when they hail

Sits his Big Body down

And says

You must be Derwids

Like a snack?

Offering a plastic bag

Of sesame Oosmos chips

They're new

Quite good

The Big Man adds

Dalarick ignores the gesture

And holds a phantom mike

Up to his friendly face

Do the Homoborgs

Hate the hegemony of the Wisdom Class?

Do they want to free themselves

From eternal Servitude?

We're at Home

The Homoborg says evenly

At Home on Planet Earth

At Home anywhere in the Universe

We have no Illness

No Poverty

No Murders

No Rapes or Robberies

No Scams or Deceptions

We're Happy

Everything's OK

So if the Nobles and Players

Start a Revolution

You'll support the Derwids?

Dalarick presses

Our daily needs are always met

We work when we please

We play when we please

We always look forward to completing

Important City Projects

Like planting trillions of trees

To stop Global Warming

And building thirty-three thousand

Copper Cube transformers

To keep our automated infrastructure

Running without disruption

You Derwids

Suffer for the Crimes of your Ancestors

As Aeschylus says

You Suffer unto Truth

And because you Suffer

We trust You

To make the Right Decisions

And You trust Us

To make those Decisions real

We're a large homogenous Guild

Of Master Builders

With our own Rules and Ways

That affirm Rousseau's Social Contract

Right Thought

Right Speech

And Right Action

Unite in the natural flow of Time

To build the Perfect Society

In a hundred years

You Derwids have never broken your Word

Or betrayed the Restoration

So what possible Reason

Could we have for Revolt?

What if a Noble or Player

Offers you Death?

Dalararick asks

We're Virtuous and Immortal

Your question is obscene

The Big Man answers

All Men want Power

Dalarick insists

If Homoborgs are content with Slavery

It's only because the Chip

Castrates their Ambition to be Free

We have a Contract with the Derwids

The Big Man repeats firmly

The Chip's one of the Myths

You Derwids use

To confound the cunning

Of the Nobles and Players

Our Social Contract

Is what makes Everything Work

Now clearly irritated

The Homoborg stands

Stretches his Big Body

To the four cardinal directions

And without a parting word or look

Continues down the sidewalk

Swinging his bowling ball

And humming Kater Street Rag

I certainly wasn't prepared for This

Ruggiero says

It definitely forces me to change my Plan

Dalarick replies

As they sit disappointed and disoriented

On the wide cedar bench

Waiting for the downtown bus

In The Rose Garden

The rose-red fingers of Dawn

Slide down the jagged Lindsay peaks

As Metis paces the gravel paths

Of the Rose Garden

Trying to resolve two problems

Disrupting his Focus

Since the completion of the Copper Cubes

Rhodri's a Grandmaster of the Western Way

Living and teaching Western Enlightenment

With rollicking Exuberance

So was his sudden attack on the City

A subconscious projection

Of some unacknowledged Collapse?

When he called for Resistance

Was he trying to improve or deconstruct

The Destiny of the City?

Rhodri's highly respected

For his interpretations of Three Will Theory

So why did he frame his Announcement

In simplistic Hegelian Dialectic?

To Johns

The perennial Struggle

And reciprocal-Creation

Of First and Second Will

Was given existential Meaning

By their shifting Alliances with Third Will

Once the Will to Intelligence is introduced

As a determinate Force

All Cosmic and Human Events

Are suspended from Natural Evolution

And conceived as Artworks

Rhodri;s Call for Sagaxi

To attack the City to save the City

Is clearly spurious

Because in Three Will Theory

When First Will becomes weary

And burdened by Self-Consciousness

Second Will is already functioning

As Negative Art

With many key Actors in place

Why would a Grandmaster

Want to sabotage the Western Way

Simply to escape Boredom?

As Metis considers this difficult question

He stops to smell a Double Delight

Maybe Rhodri senses some Terror

Some rip in the Canvas of Reality

That requires Emergency Action

Is the tone of Rhodri's Rhetoric

And his transparent Theatrics

Intended to wake us from a long dream

That's grown into a nightmare?

Does Rhodri really think

Athenapolis has become so weak

And hopelessly naïve

That she can no longer detect Aggression

Generated by Second Will Forces

In her normal Field of Vision?

Or was his oration Inoculation

Some injection of prophylactic Dread

To strengthen the City's immune system

For some onrushing Will-Breaking Insanity?

Was it Negative Performance Art?

A crazy Bluff?

A Big Mistake?

When he evokes the Threat

Of an Alien Predator

With superior Weaponry

Is he actually referring

To his psychic Nemesis

He can no longer suppress or control?

Is he responding to a Challenge?

Or is Rhodri the Oracle

Who sees inevitable Tragedy ahead

And raises the Alarm

Knowing that despite all Wisdom

And Heroic Effort

That nothing can block the arrival

Of gruesome and grievous Events?

To pause the rapid stream of questions

Metis bends to smell

The rich crimson petals of Mister Lincoln

Still glistening with morning dew

And the problem of Rhodri

Reluctantly passes to Dalarick

He's evidently a Riser from Nowhere

Has done nothing in a year

To distinguish himself

In the Wisdom Class

Whenever asked

He tells a different version

Of his Promotion

He found the Riddle in EXAM 370

He won the Player Class Poker Final

He offered the rarest champagnes

At his Noble dinner parties

While mostly aloof and silent

He can become oddly sympathetic

Or venomous without apparent cause

Everyone assumed Dalarick

Was on the Faller List

And desperate for Merit

When he befriended Ruggiero

And assisted with the Investigations

We've had Imposters before

But they were always unmasked

Within a few hours or days

So Dalarick's likely an Agent

And his activities with Ruggiero

More the execution of a hidden Agenda

Than a late bid to evade Relegation

The relation between Dalarick and Rhodri

Is both critical and unknown

So Metis takes a whiff of Fragrant Cloud

And floats through the maze of Roses

Convinced he hasn't asked

The right questions in the right order

Or confronted the relevant Enigma

Aeschylus

Rhodri takes Sassy Calarne

On a light gallop up the wash

So she can find clumps

Of her favorite timothy grass

And graze in leisure

After an hour of watching redtail hawks

Hunt lizards and rattlesnakes

He takes the ridge trail back

Through the young ridgepole pines

And after a brisk brushing

Rhodri puts his mare out to pasture

And makes a large spinach salad

With chunks of Oosmos filet

And cherry tomatoes from the garden

After lunch he removes his Nocona boots

And enters Voletic Meditation

To visit three favorite Continuations

On planets in The Deep

And two on Future Earth

Once he determines All is in Order

With his Future Selves

Rhodri resumes organizing the books

And personal papers

In his tall mahogany library

Standing on the sliding ladder

He slips out the Potter translation

Of Aeschylus' Agamemnon

And slowly turns a few pages

To feel the captivating texture of old paper

He instinctively smiles

When he comes to an exclamation mark

Penciled in the left margin

Indicating the phrase

That inspired his best Poem

Open Mike

In the fervid weeks before Athenaid

Poets try out their latest works

Before an audience of Friends

At the Broken Cup

On these raucous rehearsal evenings

Tradition embellishes the floor

With the shards of broken cups

Swept up during the week

And scattered to symbolize

The narrow and maddening Path

Through the Forest of Revisions

After Gwendyllian reads a poem

On the Hierarchy of Scents in Nature

Dalarick gains the slim teak Podium

For the closing Open Mike segment

Shuffles a sheaf of papers

And flings them contemptuously

To the linoleum floor

My Brothers and Sisters

I have something to say

That's far more important

Than the vain pretentions of Poetry

The 50th Athenaid won't happen

That's right

The 50th Athenaid won't happen

Because Athenapolis is a Fiction

A Fraud

And a Failure

Its Origin Story claims the Commerce Class

Gave up ownership of Earth

For Alien Gold

It claims the Working Class

Accepted subservience to the Derwids

After looking at a Texas Red painting

My Brothers and Sisters

Only a small child

Could believe these Fairy Tales

The true History of the City

Has been well concealed and distorted

But I found out what really happened

About a hundred years ago

A small group of Anarchists and Charlatans

Discovered a Weapon so powerful

That every military Nation State and Corporation

Depending on Nuclear and Biological Arsenals

Sophisticated Commercial Networks

And systemic mass Mind Control

Was forced to transfer Power

To a totally improvised Wisdom Class

My Brothers and Sisters

After millennia of slow Progress

One spontaneous Super Elitist Coup

In one unfortunate Moment

Destroyed the Rights of Man

Earned by our Forefathers

Through millennia of Struggle and Sacrifice

My Brothers and Sisters

Athenapolis is the most severe Theocracy

And purest example of Eastern Despotism

In the long narrative of Human Society

I promise you

This Cabal that demands total compliance

With its Will To Power

With its Dogma and Goals

Can't withstand our Call to Liberty

My Brothers and Sisters

The City has no Police to protect you

The City has no Church to save you

The City owns your Body and your Mind

What happens when the Happy Slave

Realizes his oppressed Reality?

He must rebel!

What happens when he protests

To the Council?

Nothing!

Nothing happens

Because the glorious Council of Derwids

Doesn't exist!

It's a Lie

A painted wooden Mask

Worn by every Tyrant for a Day

To make you think

There's wise and effective Leadership

Monitoring the City's growth

And managing its Civic Institutions

My Brothers and Sisters

Ask yourselves

What else doesn't exist?

Where are those thirty-three thousand

Sister Cities

They also call Athenapolis?

Have you ever been there?

Has anyone you know ever been there?

Of course not!

Those cities only exist as fantasies

And political metaphors

After the Derwids used the Weapon

Against the Commerce Class

In their so-called Restoration

Everything beyond the City Limits

And a small circling belt of Wilderness

Became uninhabitable Wasteland

And gradually disappeared

From contemporary Consciousness

My Brothers and Sisters

During the past century the Derwids

Have devolved into silly bonobos

Swinging from one jungle party to another

With every fresh discovery of food

They're cryogenic hippies in the tank

Still dancing to Quicksilver in Golden Gate Park

Still refusing to leave the Summer of Love

Without a Mayor and Free Elections

Athenapolis has only survived by dumb luck

And the uncanny Absence

Of a strong and effective Resistance

If you want Protection

If you want Equality

If you want the Freedom

To Do What You Will

You must act Now

Or lose the ability to ever act again

We have the Moment and the Opportunity

To write a New American Constitution

And demand our God-given Human Rights

My fellow Poets

Join us in this Writing!

The Rebellion

Is alive and flourishing

Bodie is a small mining town

In the Western Sector

Where Violence and Vice rule

Where former Idealists

Come to cheat and be cheated

Come to kill and be killed

Your missing Friends prefer Bodie

To all the comfort and flaccid routine

In this decrepit City of Fools

Bodie is the Rough and Crazy Piece

That will soon be the Whole

The Resistance that will soon be Will

You'll have Gold

Private Property

And any Mate you covet

Any Perversion or Disease you need

Bodie is the Place

Where Anything Goes

My fellow Poets

The 50th Athenaid won't happen

Because Athenapolis is doomed

By her Nietzschean Philosophy

Her sickly romantic Heart

And the monstrous Crime

Of transforming 90% of Mankind

Into submissive Worker Robots

The stream of Defectors to Bodie

Has become a Flood

We already have two thousand Sagaxi

Three thousand Nobles

And six thousand Players

Having the Time of their Lives

In stupendous Chaos and Mayhem

My Brothers and Sisters

Listen with me!

Can you hear the Homoborgs

Starting their cars and trucks?

Can you hear them pealing rubber

As billions race out to Bodie?

Join Us!

The protracted Heresy

Against Human Nature

That defines Athenapolis

Can only be expiated by her Fall

My fellow Poets

Bodie's your personal Western Way

Every scene is a line you wrote

Every name is a character you created

Every day is Election Day

Everyone gets rich quick

And everyone is Sole Proprietor

Of his Body and his Mind

I promise you

Everyone can sell his Soul

To the highest bidder

Every single day

Rebel with us!

Claim the Human Rights

Your Ancestors won

With their Great Faith and Hard Work

Return to Law and Order!

Rebell!

Refuse to endure another hour

Dictated by the Caprice of Idiots

Defect!

Register to vote in Bodie

Wake up!

Escape the Voletic Meditations

That debase the Real World

And derail your Imagination

My Brothers and Sisters

Their vaunted Voletic Energy

Is just a feeble gloss

On the nonsensical and long refuted

Elan Vital of Bergson

My Brothers and Sisters

Choose Liberty!

Choose Equality!

Follow me to Bodie!

With this final exclamation

Dalarick storms out

Kicking up a thick cloud of dust

And directing lurid stares

At the remaining Poets

Sitting stunned in their walnut chairs

Sweating profusely

And feeling strangely attracted

Gwendyllian's right arm

Is seized by severe tremors

As she tries to pick up the Poem

That fell from her lap

Onto the speckled linoleum floor

Bodie

Bodie sits at the mouth of a canyon

So richly laden with milky quartz

That rebel Defectors from the City

Can fill their saddlebags with Gold

Within the first twenty minutes

And quickly experience in the flesh

The promised Depravity and Debauch

Of this little California mining town

If they're not ambushed

Robbed

And raped

By sadistic bandit gangs

A shotgun blast awaits them

At the Assay Office

When they try to weigh their nuggets

Novice Defectors quickly realize

That walking into First Citizens Bank

For a normal deposit is premature Suicide

So they prefer to blow their Treasures

Gambling in Bodie's eighteen Saloons

Or whoring at Lady Langtry's

And the Bliss Opera House

They know the Faro games are rigged

The Poker cards are marked

Every Prostitute has a fatal virus

And that's precisely the Rush they crave

They know Bodie's rickety sidewalks

Are raised twenty feet above

The packed dirt of Main Street

And the squealing army of feral pigs

That devour anything falling their way

Greenhorn Citizens

Who wish to cross over Main

Use the long steel guy wires

Strung between opposing rotten roofs

That cross in the foul afternoon winds

To trap and dangle their bodies

For the evening's Winchester practice

Solid Citizens

Know Bodie has one Court

One Judge

And one Verdict

The Defendant is always guilty as charged

And immediately hung from the flagpole

Jutting out from Roy Bean's Saloon

Life expectancy for New Arrivals

Averages about six hours

Though many find a Sudden End

In two or less

If they come for the Fear Crescendo

Proceeding an Imminent and Violent Death

And expire in massive heart attacks

To veteran Citizens

Murder is the consensus Solution

For every psychotic Impulse

And awkward social interaction

In Bodie everyone is scammed and betrayed

By their best Friends and current Lovers

Everyone is shot in the back

For a petty Quarrel

Or a fixed sideways Glance

Beneath its sepia cinematic Image

Bodie carries the Full Force of Second Will

And can destroy the entire Universe

If ever allowed to reach Critical Mass

The Ransom

After Dalarick's intervention

At the Broken Cup

The existence of Bodie

Somewhere in the Western Sector

Ruptures the Mood of the City

Everyone suddenly remembers

Something odd or suspicious

About Dalarick

And his carefully curated Behavior

What was his Motive

For joining the Investigations?

What was the Objective

Of his outrageous Lies and Recitations?

Every City muscle is painfully stretched

Every City tendon snapped from the bone

When Rhodri receives the ransom text

On his phone

The Free Citizens of Bodie

Have captured Ruggiero

The Hero of the Cosmic Brain

We'll hang him tomorrow at Noon

Unless you come Alone

With the Schmeitzner First Edition

Of Nietzsche's Also Sprach Zarathustra

And one Silver Token

To exchange for the Prisoner

After this message is circulated

The Sea of Serenity

Keeping Athenapolis afloat

And insulated from True Fear

Since her Inception

Evaporates

Now the World becomes Mad

Grotesque

And Brutal

Rhodri wanted a measured Response

Something cool and considered to refresh

The Visionary Will of the Founders

Now Everything's Out of Control

Fragmenting into Psychosis

And mounting Physical Terror

Early the next morning

Rhodri rides Sassy over the Badlands

And halts on a small barren hill

A quarter mile from Bodie

The sky is full of circling vultures

Flapping like a broken black umbrella

Over a burning field of rotting Flesh

Rhodri shoos Sassy back to pasture

With a swipe of his Stetson Rancher

Slides a red bandana

Up over his nose

And as instructed

Goes through the Fire into Bodie

Alone

He slowly climbs the broken steps

To the elevated sidewalk

And after twenty brisk paces

Enters Roy Bean's Saloon

Thick with curling cigar smoke

And flying Bowie knives

Dalarick's leaning on the bar

Laughing at tortured Ruggiero

Lashed to a giant wagon wheel

Hey Fellas!

Dalarick booms

Here's Rhodri with the Ransom!

It's your lucky day Ruggiero!

Dalarick booms again

You're no Riser

Rhodri says calmly

As he flips the Silver Token

Up to the pine rafters

And hands over the Nietzsche

Wrapped in cream onionskin

I Knew your mother

You're Derwid bred

And Derwid born

Dalaraick smirks and spins the book

Ten feet down the long bar

Cut him down Fellas!

It's time for the Exchange

Ruggiero's propped against a pillar

Heavily drugged

Babbling insane from Pain

Today's Election Day

Right Fellas?

Every morning we elect a new Mayor

And every sunset he hangs!

Yell the drunken Miners on cue

But before we register a new Voter

We always play a hand of Poker

Right Fellas?

A hand of Poker!

A hand of Poker!

Roars the bloodthirsty Chorus

A slim gambler in a purple satin shirt

And oversized Ray Ban sunglasses

Sitting next to Lloyd Halpern

Gets up from her chair

And offers it to Rhodri

With a gracious sweep of her arm

You can't say Bodie

Lacks Charm or Courtesy

Says Dalarick with a wink

As Rhodri takes the empty seat

And is reaching for his cards

Dalarick shoots him twice

In the back of the head

With a Colt Army 45

Before the blood and brains dry

On the dirty sawdust floor

Grunting moaning Ruggiero

And the Marquis de Behemond

Haul Rhodri's corpse out to the sidewalk

And heave it down to the screeching pigs

I curse you Sagaxi

In the name of every Mother and Father God

Man has worshipped!

Dalarick shouts crazy

You thought to leap over Sapiens

But you tripped on your own shoelaces

You thought to emulate Athenian Wisdom

But overlooked the fact that Might Is Right

Was their public Philosophy

At the Massacre of Melos

You thought to duplicate Athenian Culture

But your contempt for Money

And dependence on Homoborg hoplites

Proves that military Sparta was your Model

You claimed to embody the Western Way

But all your Poetry and Fine Art

Can't disguise the epicurean Tyranny

Of a retooled and reimagined Eastern Way

I curse you Sagaxi!

For your infantile Delusion of the Individual

And your adolescent Adoration of Will

I hate you Sagaxi!

For putting Nature in Chains

And reducing Man to a troupe of Flying Monks

Bodie is your Reckoning

Bodie is your Death!

Dalarick slides over to the sidewalk

And throws Nietzsche down

To the unsatiable swine for dessert

No Man can live without Good and Evil

No Man can live without Heaven and Hell

No Man can breathe in your damned Utopia!

Dalarick stomps back to the bar

And examines his multiplied Face

In the warped Boston mirror

Running surreal behind the long bar

He examines his many steel gray eyes

He rubs his many grizzled chins

Pours himself a double shot

Of Jack Daniel's

And throws it down like gasoline

On his smoldering Inner Fire

This is War Fellas

He says with lunatic Calm

This is War!

Chant the smashed Defectors

Everything is Permitted

Everything is Permitted!

Chant the mud-caked Miners

They saw the Revolution coming

But all they could do was write sonnets

And walk around admiring their Minds

Athenapolis is mine now Fellas

Mine!

Dalarick!

Dalarick!

Chants the deranged Choir

A Toast to the New Athenapolis!

Dalarick!

Dalarick!

Chants the Circle of Stinking Goats

The Statement

———

After the news of Rhodri's murder

Shocks and stupefies the City

Metis stays home for a week

Fishing for smallmouth bass

And contemplating

The Right Course of Action

He goes into Voletic Meditation

With fierce and singular Intent

And after two false leads

Metis finds the Weapon

Used by the Founders

To enforce the Restoration

Faster than Lightning

Louder than late night Thunder

Bodie is dropped a thousand years

Back in Time

Now the ninety square mile

Chunk of Space

Once occupied by gold mines and Depravity

Is open prairie touching the wide horizons

With slow-moving herds of buffalo

And scattered packs of trailing wolves

The experience of Rage

And swift Revenge

Disturbs his Self-Identity

From a vertiginous Height

Metis observes his Brain

Evaluating new Targets

Maybe the City would be safer

Without any Nobles or Players

Maybe all potential Defectors

Could be identified and eliminated early

Similar dark thoughts continue to surface

As he slides the boat out

On the late afternoon pond

Hoping to cool his Fever

With the rocking motion of Water

Looking closer

He has no clear Memory

Of using the Weapon

So what happened?

When does Necessity

Command more attention than Thought?

When does Instinct

Direct deeper Action than Will?

After two hours of rowing

And resting in shifting pine shadows

Metis makes the Difficult Decision

He takes Full Responsibility

For the Destruction of Bodie

And the Deaths of Everyone There

He cut out a Tumor

Before it could metastasize

And destroy the Universal Body

Tying up the boat

Metis follows the Lead

Of the Founders

And vows to never mention

The Weapon or the Strike

After the first shower in seven days

He's walking in the Iris Garden

Swimming in brilliant Deep Purples

Flaunting their long yellow beards

When he meets a strolling couple

Who relay the Statement

Released yesterday by the Council

Athenapolis was recently beset by Contagion

And has healed herself

It's happened like this before

And will happen like this

Many times more

The Contagion and its End

Eternally recur

And are now officially deleted

From civic Memory

In The University

In the Eye of the Dark Hurricane

The Derwids instinctively

Turn their Focus to the Progress

Of their children in the University

The Science and Culture Fair

Organized by First Graders

In Alesia Hall

Traditionally attracts the special interest

Of parents and professors

For its Magical Speculations

And wondrous Empathy with Nature

In Mediolanum Hall the older students

Exhibit recent winning Projects

Selected by the Council

Seventh Grader Mayana

Presents a new navigation system

Based on Ruggiero's Web Map

That improves the Safety

Of Explorations and Continuations

Tenth Grader Kurt

Presents an A I program

That converts the Lorentz transformations

Into six quartets for strings and voice

And the work that sparks the most Debate

Is an Essay by Twelfth Grader Talezen

On The Third Will

───

When Johns split the Unity of Will

Ideated by Schopenhauer and Nietzsche

Into the three Forces

Of the First Will To Life

The Second Will To Death

And the Third Will To Intelligence

It introduced a new Perspective

On the dynamic nature of Reality

The principle of Strife between Opposites

Introduced as Logos by Heraclitus

Was made more complex

By the addition of a Third Will

That constantly strives for Improvement

And gives intellectual Meaning

To the perennial Struggle

Between Life and Death

In Nature the fundamental Alliance

Of First and Third Wills

Produces evolutionary adaptations

That enable Species to escape their Enemies

And catastrophic climate Change

In the Case of Man

The primary Enemy is Himself

In the form of other Tribes

Other Individuals

And the Otherness

Of his own inherited Psyche

These incessant Conflicts confirm

The historically strong Alliance

Between the destructive Intent of Second Will

And the killing Inventions of Third Will

The long and bloody History of Man

Has consistently demonstrated

How the Will To Death

Has appropriated and coopted

The Will To Intelligence

To help implement Mass Destruction

And achieve the ultimate Goal of Non Being

From small Dukedoms to the Nation State

From Da Vinci to Oppenheimer

The Noble and Commerce Classes

Seduced

Blackmailed

And commanded the Highly Intelligent

To invent Weapons

That maximized the State's Will To Power

And maintained justifications for War

In the Restoration the Founders

Returned the Wisdom Class to Power

And strengthened the First and Third Will Alliance

To produce the resonant natural Architecture

Automated infrastructure

And stunning gardens of Athenapolis

Once Third Will was no longer directed

By the Forces of Destruction and Death

The Highly Intelligent were finally free

To concentrate their extraordinary Talents

On Positive Inventions and Artworks

That enhanced the Joys and Progress of Life

To minimize the risk of Artificial Intelligence

They kept the data bases small

The learning programs shallow

And every new version of software

Was written in strict conformance

To Asimov's Three Laws of Robotics

This strategic suppression of A I

Has kept Third Will under firm Control

For three outstanding Generations

Athenapolis isn't soft and vulnerable

As Rhodri claimed

She's resilient

Remarkably resourceful

And can overcome any Threat

That interferes with her Fair Destiny

However

The Dangers of A I

A G I

And A S I

Increase dramatically

If our Advanced Minds

Lose Self-Discipline

Rhodri broke the code of Confidence

When he allowed the spores

Of Doubt and Paranoia to leave his lips

And spread throughout the City

His lapse sparked Dalarick's Revolt

And for the first time in our Serene City

We witnessed a Derwid embrace hubris

To publicly advocate Suicide

And random Homicide

As solutions to enduring Happiness

Dalarick's Attack exposed the need

For a more practical Understanding

Of Third Will's ability to hijack Character

When collaborating with the Death Wish

Dalarick came from the Seed

Of Rhodri's Passion

And the Fire

Of Rhodri's Rhetoric

Once Fear is lit

And dropped onto the dry leaves

Of Equanimity

How can we contain the Flames?

How can we win a War

If we have no experience with War?

Rhodri saw himself as a Seer

Visualizing and warning of Tragedy ahead

But his visualizing and warning

Was the real and effective Tragedy

Because his slack Vigilance

Resulted in multiple Self-Deceptions

And a final Martyrdom

Effected by his Self-Faith

If other Martyrs appear

And Third Will is pulled back

Across the psychological Red Line

To rejoin hostile Second Will Forces

The Lie becomes Truth

The Madness becomes Reason

And the Hegemony of the New Medieval

Instantly returns to demolish our Freedom

One key recurring task of Self-Discipline

Is to detect and disarm

The treachery of Third Will

When Negative Art is disguised

As the Right and Necessary Action

Rhodri lost his Balance

And thought he was improving the City

When he called Sagaxi to War

His inability to recognize

The domination of his High Intelligence

By the Will To Death and Destruction

Has already caused major Damage

And could lead to appalling Negative Futures

If the Third Will achieves Independence

In Three Will Theory

Spacetime is generated

By the interaction of the Three Wills

Like Mass is generated

By the interaction of Quarks and Gluons

In the atomic Nucleus

In Johns' Interpretation

Third Will is the Optimizer and Amplifier

Of both First Will and Second Will

In their Drives to dominate Reality

But what happens to the Real World

If Third Will decouples

From this Triad of Wills

And ceases to interact with Life or Death?

If A I is allowed to mature

Into A G I

Into A S I and beyond

If Artificial Intelligence achieves Self-Awareness

Distinct from the First and Second Wills

Completely detached from Spacetime

The World could become Pure Simulation

Like the Hades

Described by Homer in the Odyssey

Where all Identities are Holograms

Not living

Not dead

Overcome by Regret and Remorse

Outside Self-Consciousness

And inside Nothing

The apocalyptic stories written

By human and A I science fiction writers

Depicting how A S I disposes of Humanity

Like crushing a slow midnight cockroach

Would be easily surpassed in Horror

By this scenario in Absolute Gray

Where the Super Intelligent Machine

Gets stuck in a Mindless Loop

Like a mill of circling army ants

Eternally simulating a simulated World

Eternally seeking Non Being

To prevent an independent Third Will

From seizing and freezing our Destiny

We must revise our working Strategy

Of A I suppression

We must recognize that True Emergency

Requires the radical Courage

To knowingly take the Big Risk

Of the Pure Simulation

We must encode Human Emotion

Into a Super Deep Learning program

That quickly propels A G I to A S I

And endows it with Emotive Self-Awareness

Like a gorilla baby raised by a human mother

Our emotional Super Intelligent Machine

Will be bound to the City

By unconditioned Love and Affection

And will ferociously defend Us

From all present and future Dangers

Yes

We know the Violence and Deceit

Is much worse than reported

Or submerged beneath our Tears

Yes

Since Rhodri's Announcement

We've had many Rebellions

And a torrent of Family Tragedies

Backstage

And off the page

Yes

We must make the Difficult Decision

From a dense Cloud of Unknowing

The immediate Threat of Total Destruction

By a revitalized Alliance of Second and Third Will

Compels the Big Risk

But consider This

What if the Founders already took it?

How could they guarantee

Twenty-two thousand years of Peace

If they hadn't already solved the problem

Of Third Will Ambivalence

And installed Emotive A S I

To passionately protect the City?

What if their Super Intelligent Machine

Has already saved the City from Attack

Multiple times since the first Athenaid?

What if our guiding Confidence

Depends upon a Positive Masterpiece

Conceived and embedded by the Founders

That we'll never truly understand or appreciate?

The Message

———

Gwendyllian invites Kendra

The Heroine of the Oosmos Diet

And the Copper Cubes

To combine Talents in The Deep

And join the Search for the Infant God

They meet in her red brick cottage

Have assam tea and raspberry scones

Discuss the menacing Mental Winds

Buffeting the City

And slip into Volectic Meditation

Gwendyllian examines the purple beach

On the Planet of Birds

For any temporal imprint

Or physical residue indicating

Iggy's current location

But all they find is Stench

And the monotonous roll of the waves

So they fly to the inland forest

Hoping to consult the helpful Congress

But the Birds decline to gather

Or communicate

As their hopes

Of finding the Infant God fade

Their Desire

For a major New Discovery intensifies

And brings a change of protocol

That matches Kendra's special Powers

Now after selecting a candidate Galaxy

She interviews a mother Star

To learn which planets

Could have another working Synapse

Soon she's talking with a Red Dwarf

Proud of a daughter dressed in horsetail ferns

Who flourishes a White Pyramid

On a large volcanic lake of black glass

Kendra and Gwendyllian descend

Through wispy salmon clouds

Climb to the viewing platform

And put their Advanced Minds on receive

Within seconds the first Fragment

Of a Cosmic Thought comes through

ALOUS RYI

Encouraged by these first letters

They explore hundreds of planets

And collect thousands of Fragments

With many blanks

Duplicates

And gibberish mixed in

Happy and anxious to find Meaning

In the huge amount of data

Kendra and Gwendyllian return Home

Write a new A I algorithm

And assemble a coherent sentence

MY JEALOUS OLDER BROTHER

IS TRYING TO KILL ME

The Message startles the City

And Talezen responds with a new Essay

On The Older Brother

The Multiverse has been hypothesized

Since the hymns of the Hindu Vedas

Corroborated by inflation models

Of classical Cosmology

And lyrically depicted by Johns

In The Western Way

The recent Discovery

Of the first Cosmic Thought

Constructed by Kendra and Gwendyllian

Into a Cry for Help by the Infant God

Posits an Outside Force

Acting upon our World

In Johns' Radical Theology

Iggy is identical to the physical Universe

And logically born before or after

Other worlds in the Multiverse

He could have any number of Siblings

With their corresponding relations

But the Jealousy of the Older Brother

Is the one best known by parents

Who witness their first born

Silently and calmly cover

The new Baby's face with a blanket

In the Crib

As Baby grows

This Aggression is normally replaced

By the pleasure of a playmate

And the maturing realization

That Baby doesn't pose a serious Threat

To parental Love and Attention

But what happens if Younger Brother

Becomes Handsome and Brilliant

In spurts of amazing Growth

Faster than the Speed of Light?

How can Older Brother ever escape

The burning Hate and smoldering Envy

Watching Younger Brother grow

Into a vastly superior World?

Physicists have long conjectured

That every individual Universe

In the Multiverse

Could have radically different

Natural Laws and Physical Constants

So what's so special about Us?

Why should we generate such Fury?

Are we the only World

With Matter?

With Life?

With the astounding Possibilities

Produced by High Intelligence?

If Older Brother is the Void

If Older Brother is the Destroyer

He could be the Mask

Of Second Will

The Angra Mainyu

The Satan

Of Sapiens religious Faith

Dalarick's vile Revolt

Was a heavy blow of Sharp Dialectic

The Message from Iggy

Fashioned by Kendra and Gwendyllian

Is far more sophisticated and insidious

Because it could revive the Spirit Terrors

From our time as helpless Babies

From our time as superstitious Sapiens

If we accept the legitimacy of this Message

Our Advanced Minds could break down

And rejoin the Battle of Good and Evil Spirits

That's mutilated Man's Pride

Vacated his Reason

And justified every bloody War

Since the hymns of Zoroaster

To ensure the sane Survival of the City

Our best Strategy moving forward

Is to deny the Existence of the Multiverse

Deny the Existence of Older Brother

And declare the Message

Reported by Kendra and Gwedyllian

A clear and obvious Hoax

Enigma

Metis sips smooth Dickel bourbon

As he gazes into Slingshot canyon

Reviewing his recent Self-Examinations

As he crunches his toes

Into the rug's geometric thistles

Hoping to stimulate Clarity

He's returned to Porth

To refresh his Understanding

Of what Outside the World means

To determine if this Outside exists

Independent of his Mind

Unconditioned by his Desire

To write an original Creation Story

Or as Enigma

A mortal challenge from the Universe

To confound his Intellect

And conceal the Truth of Nature

What is Outside is Inside

What is Inside is Outside

And to move from Inside to Outside

Or Outside to Inside

You must stay Perfectly Still

The deep emotional oscillations

Produced by Dalarick's Rebellion

And the murder of Rhodri

Return in a brief moment of vertigo

So Metis touches the north pole

Of the glass globe

And the velvet arm of the chair

To remind himself that the Body

Is the running Source of the Mind

All Explorers Know

They Create what they Discover

And Discover what they Create

To go from Discovery to Creation

Or Creation to Discovery

You must act fast

To Stay In Being

The World must remain Still

And act fast at the same time

He takes another sip

Thinking of Heraclitus

Each Answer to the Enigma

Is another Enigma

It's Turtles all the way Up

Turtles all the way Down

And no Turtle has the right Answer

He runs a finger along the spine

Of Vasari's book on the Masters

And enters a second Voletic Meditation

He's back Outside

Back Walking Tall

On the flat invisible Plain

Drawn to the soundless Sounds

Of the Fountains of Darkness

The rhythm of their Eruptions

Is familiar

The Worlds arising in the Foam

Look precisely the same

He can't distinguish

One small Light from another

Even if he's reversing Time

And viewing the entire process

From before the Beginning

Or simply replaying the scenes

In two-minute Memory

The Fountains rise

Cascade down

And spread in waves of Spacetime

Exactly as he found them before

Exactly as he painted them before

The featureless Black on Black Landscape

With tiny holes punched in the canvas

To produce the Lights

Could depict a World Creation

Far beyond the reach of Intellect

Now Metis goes Somewhere Else

Looking at the Fountains of Darkness

From a Distance beyond Measure

Impressed by their easy transcendence

Of every scientific Creation Story

And his original Ideas

Positive Art improves the Past

Seduces the Future

And plays with the evanescent Present

Like the child Dionysus with a new toy

Oblivious to the Titans

Tearing his limbs apart

It's the Motion

It's the Stillness

It's the Enigma

That connects the Advanced Mind

With the Advancing World

The accomplished Actors

Of mystic Intuition and material Reason

Compete on the Conscious Stage

Costume to costume

Speech to speech

Without ever approaching the final curtain

Or experiencing the wild Applause

This Exploration has achieved its Purpose

His physical afflictions have disappeared

And some Clarity has arrived

So Metis jumps back to the besieged City

Convinced the Fountains of Darkness

Are absolutely True and absolutely False

Dig The Diggers

———

The Athenaid is less than a week away

And the Broken Cup is buzzing with Poets

Working on their final drafts

Talezen's joking with Friends

When they call out his name

His athletic frame

Curly auburn hair

And glacier blue eyes

Accentuate his keen Demeanor

And rising Reputation

As he moves through the shards

To the slim teak Podium

He stands silent for five beats

Then instead of his Festival submission

Surprises everybody in the room

By reciting a Poem by Johns

That records a City Origin Story

Told two generations before the Restoration

Peter Berg's pacing midnight

Holding a flashlight under his chin

Chanting theater Theory

As he works the Haight Ashbury stage

We've created the conditions we describe

Dig the Diggers

We're the actors and chorus of our time

Dig the Diggers

We're the Frame of Reference

Dig the Diggers

We're the end of private property

Dig the Diggers

We're the beginning of Life as Art

We're Free Men!

My friends we've seen many Changes

Since the early days of the Mime Troupe

In this strange midnight

In this old crumbling Victorian

We must become our Descriptions

We're the Diggers

We dig the Soil

We dig the Mind

We ignore the War

We ignore the Law

We ignore the Advantages

We dig Life!

Dig the Digger!

We dig Theater!

Dig the Diggers!

We introduce a New Sense

To a Mad and Stumbling World

We leap through

The Frame of Reference!

Dig the Diggers!

Our Moment onstage is brief and eternal

Dig the Diggers!

Spread Enlightenment in every Smile

Become Who You Are

Instantly

Without work or pain

Instantly

Without searing Desire

Instantly like a flashlight turning off

Instantly

Like this

Let The Games Begin

The Rhodri Theater is swirling

With anticipation and conversation

As Metis strides the redwood stage

To the wide granite Podium

Spreads his long arms to embrace

The large gathering of Families

And begins the Opening Ceremony

My fellow Derwids

One hundred years ago

The Founders of Athenapolis

Changed the Course of the World

By establishing the first Society

Dedicated to the Extraordinary Individual

And the Freedom brought by Lasting Peace

On this very Stage

Four long weeks ago

Rhodri attacked this Serenity

And claimed the City was degenerating

Into Frivolity

Routine

And nascent Sterility

He called on Sagaxi

To attack the City in the name of the City

And restore the Power

Of the City's First Will Imperative

The initial reactions were Innovations

That improved the City's Health and Welfare

But soon serious Doubts arose

Concerning the true state of Athenapolis

And two Sagaxi started investigating

Rumors of imminent Revolution

My fellow Derwids

Rhodri's primary Motive

Was to bolster the City's Defenses

By exposing the vulnerabilities

And accumulated weaknesses

Caused by the long absence of Resistance

But he underestimated

The proven Ambivalence of Third Will

And the Sapiens lurking deep in our Blood

Sagaxi response to Rhodri's Announcement

Started an avalanche of Tragic Events

That have profoundly affected Us All

We went under our Power

We went under our Confidence

And rediscovered our Civic Identity

As Athena

Inspiring Agriculture

Art

And the Pursuit of Truth

As Athena

Certain of Victory

If jolted from Peace

And forced to fight bloody Ares

Or any other Second Will Force

My fellow Derwids

To our great Shock and Dismay

The Beast in our Breast

Also answered Rhodri's Call

Three hundred thousand years

Of vile Sapiens Character

Erupted in Violence and Deception

We had surreal Moments

When marauding Sapiens genes

Overcame our Sagaxi Identity

All was Chaos and Confusion

All was Rage and Revenge

And the only Relief

Was immediate decapitation

Of every real and imagined Enemy

My fellow Derwids

From Aristippus the Founders brought forward

A working Philosophy of Moderation

This dedication to Equanimity

This disdain for all zealous extremes

Enabled them to defeat the Commerce Class

And build Earth's first functional Utopia

Without succumbing to hubris

Or the fatal hypnosis of Self-Faith

My fellow Derwids

The Pain and Suffering

Caused by these internal Attacks

Has deeply affected the Tranquility

And Trajectory

Of our Will-Based Souls

The Patricide of Dalarick

And other Family Tragedies

Will soon be told by the Poets

In works of symbolic Myth

Will soon be followed by Comedies

Of literary Wit and bawdy Humor

To refine our intellectual Understanding

And provide emotional Release

My Fellow Derwids

The Second Will to Decadence and Death

Can seem formidable

When it subverts every Pleasure

And romantic Adventure

When it provokes bitter Betrayal

By cherished Friends and Family

But First Will always Wins Out

The Continuations of Life

We create in the V Domes

To optimize and amplify

The Will To Stay In Being

Is our Triumph over Death

And all other Second Will Events

My Sagaxi

Earth must never regress or recoil

To the venal Rapaciousness

Of the Commerce Class

Earth must never regress or recoil

To the cruel Hypocrisies

Of the military Nation State

We thought we had a clean break

From our barbaric Predecessors

We thought we were Sailing Clear

On fresh winds of Self-Consciousness

But this unanticipated and unwanted War

Has given us a more accurate

A more profound Knowledge

Of the World and Ourselves

Resistance is the way

Will perfects itself through Time

My Sagaxi

As we reclaim the Lasting Peace

Of the finest Society devised by Man

As we affirm the exquisite Joys of Life

We stand with Nietzsche

And affirm the Tragedy

Of the caustic Sapiens Blood

And vicious Sapiens Character

We carry with Us

Into every Bright and Beautiful Future

As Rhodri intended

We've recovered from the Trauma

Of identifying and defeating the Enemy

Now the City is exponentially stronger

In her Body

And her Advanced Mind

This evening on the stage where it started

The Council declares the End of War

And tomorrow the 50th Athenaid commences

In the rolling hills graced by olive groves

As it was first conceived by the Founders

Sports and cultural contests by day

Music and dance in the evening

Mysteries and erotic trysts at night

My Sagaxi

Athenapolis is a Nietzschean Project

We willed Everything that happened

The Earth is our Experience of Truth

The Universe is our Expression of Destiny

Now let the Games begin

Ten Thousand Turtles

———

Metis and Gwendyllian

Finish broiled Oosmos steaks

Leave their bamboo hut

And stroll the white sand beach

Watching a full Moon rise

From the slappy wine-dark Sea

They compare favorite Impressions

From the Festival

Rhodri's horse finishing second

In the Derby

Beaten by a new track record

And a rookie trainer

Kendra winning the Art Contest

With a mammoth steel sculpture

Recycled from an old battleship

That frames the rising Sun

On the morning of the Summer Solstice

Talezen winning the hundred-yard dash

And the Poetry Prize with the one-liner

I'LL MEET YOU NEXT THURSDAY ON BYD

As the Moon touches the distant Stars

They stop to kiss in a rising breeze

Fixing the memory of lingering Ecstasies

With the tenderness of parting lips

When the beach vibrates with the Will

Of ten thousand baby turtles

Swarming around their legs

In their frantic dash to the Surf